THE PUPPY PLACE

BAXTER

THE PUPPY PLACE

**Don't miss any of these
other stories by Ellen Miles!**

THE PUPPY PLACE

BAXTER

ELLEN MILES

SCHOLASTIC INC.

New York   Toronto   London   Auckland
Sydney   Mexico City   New Delhi   Hong Kong

For Matt (aka Mr. Popper), with gratitude for his support and guidance.

Special thanks to Steve and Chris for introducing me to their incredible dogs.

ISBN 978-0-545-21798-9

Cover art by Tim O'Brien
Original cover design by Steve Scott

13 12   13 14 15/0

Printed in the U.S.A.   40

First printing, June 2010

CHAPTER ONE

"Doesn't Buddy look adorable sitting there? He's so good." Lizzie clasped her hands and smiled at her puppy. "Good boy, Buddy!"

Buddy cocked his head and thumped his tail. Then he jumped up and took a step toward Lizzie.

Lizzie held up her hand. "No, Buddy. Stay. Wait until the photographer takes the picture!"

Buddy started to sit again, but then he couldn't seem to help himself. He bounded over to Lizzie, put his paws on her lap, and stretched up to lick her face. Lizzie couldn't help herself, either. She giggled and hugged him tightly. "Buddy! You're supposed to be getting your picture taken. That means you have to sit still."

Buddy squirmed and kept licking, and Lizzie laughed some more. Who could be mad at a puppy as cute as Buddy, with his soft brown fur and the white spot in the shape of a heart, right in the middle of his chest? How was he supposed to know that this portrait session was a very special treat? If Buddy would only let the photographer take his picture, Lizzie and the rest of her family would have a fantastic photo to keep forever. The Petersons all loved Buddy so much.

Lizzie's family fostered puppies, which meant that they took care of puppies who needed homes, just until they could find each one the perfect forever family. Buddy had started out as a foster puppy, but he had ended up becoming part of the Peterson family. Lizzie could not have been happier about that. Her younger brothers Charles and the Bean both loved Buddy, too.

Now Lizzie had managed to get Buddy to sit still again. "Sorry," she said as soon as she stopped laughing long enough to catch her breath.

"It's okay," said the photographer, a pretty Japanese-American woman named Katana. She shook back her long black hair and smiled. "I'm used to it. I'm still setting up, anyway. I'll let you know when I'm really ready."

Lizzie was at Bowser's Backyard, her aunt Amanda's doggy day-care center. Aunt Amanda was even crazier about dogs than Lizzie (if that was even possible), so the business was perfect for her. She took care of people's dogs while their owners were at work or on vacation. Some days she had as many as thirty dogs! Thirty *lucky* dogs. Instead of lying around alone at home, these dogs got to spend each day playing, napping, eating homemade dog treats, and enjoying activities like doggy crafts, doggy games, and even doggy massages. The luckiest dogs of all got to spend weekends with Aunt Amanda and Uncle

James up at their country place, Camp Bowser. There the dogs could swim, romp in the woods, play doggy Frisbee, or just nap on the porch.

Lizzie loved to help out at Bowser's Backyard, although lately she had not had the chance. Aunt Amanda had not needed any extra help for a few weeks — but she sure did today. Today was Picture Day. A professional photographer — Katana — had come to take pictures of Aunt Amanda's regular customers. Most of the owners had been happy to sign up, even though these special portraits would cost extra.

Katana had set up a plain white backdrop for the dogs to pose in front of. She had fancy lights and a big camera on a tripod and lots of dog treats and squeaky toys for getting the dogs' attention. That was Lizzie's job. When Katana raised her finger to show that she was all ready to snap a picture, Lizzie was supposed to squeeze a squeaky toy so that the dog would look up at the camera, hopefully with a cute, alert expression.

Aunt Amanda's job — not an easy one — was to get the dogs to sit still in the first place. If anybody could do it, Aunt Amanda could. She really had an almost magical way with animals. She could train any dog to do just about anything. Lizzie knew that if Aunt Amanda had been in the room, Buddy would have sat still for her. But Aunt Amanda was in the playroom, getting the other dogs ready for their pictures. Buddy was just a practice dog for Katana to experiment with before the real photo session started. Lizzie's mom had brought him along when she dropped Lizzie off, and now she was waiting patiently to take Buddy home.

"Okay," said Katana, straightening up from her camera. "I think I'm all set. Can you get Buddy to sit and stay, right there where I've taped a big X to the floor?"

Lizzie brought Buddy over to the spot and told him to sit. Buddy sat, gazing up at her hopefully.

Am I going to get a cookie for this?

"Good boy." Lizzie wished she had remembered to tuck a few of his favorite biscuits into her pocket. She smiled at Buddy and petted his head. He thumped his tail.

Pats are almost as good as cookies!

"Buddy, stay!" said Lizzie. She held up her hand, palm toward Buddy. With Aunt Amanda's help, Lizzie was just starting to teach her puppy some hand signals. Still holding up her palm, she took a few steps backward. "Good boy," she said encouragingly. "Good stay." A few more steps, and Lizzie found herself standing next to Katana. Buddy sat very, very still, but Lizzie could see that it wasn't easy for him. He was trembling a little, and his tail made tiny *thump-thump-thumps* on the floor.

Katana waved a finger. Quickly, Lizzie reached

into the toy basket and grabbed a red plastic fire hydrant. She held it up right next to the camera and gave it a big squeeze. When the toy let out a loud squeak, Buddy cocked his head and stared at the camera. *Snap.*

"Got it!" said Katana just as Buddy bolted toward Lizzie, wagging his tail wildly and giving her that special doggy grin of his. Lizzie laughed and gave him the fire hydrant to chew on. *Squeak! Squeak! Squeak-squeak-squeak!* Buddy danced around the room, tossing the toy into the air and pouncing on it over and over again.

"Perfect," said Katana. "He looked adorable. That's just how we'll do it with all of the other dogs."

Lizzie called Buddy over. "Good boy," she told him one more time, when he brought her the fire hydrant.

"I can't wait to see how the picture turns out," said Lizzie's mom as she clipped on Buddy's leash.

"Here's a peek right now," said Katana. She showed Lizzie and Mrs. Peterson the screen on her camera. There was Buddy looking his absolute cutest, with his head tilted to one side and his ears perked to perfection.

"Aww," said Mrs. Peterson.

"You're really good," Lizzie told Katana.

Katana smiled modestly. "I've taken pictures of a *lot* of dogs," she said. "It's my main business."

After her mom left to take Buddy home, Lizzie's job started for real. Aunt Amanda brought the dogs in one at a time: Hoss, a dignified Great Dane; Crackers, a cocker spaniel; Pugsley, the wild and wacky little pug Lizzie's family had fostered; and of course Bowser, Aunt Amanda's golden retriever.

Aunt Amanda got the dogs to sit. Katana adjusted her lights, focused her camera, and gave Lizzie the signal. Lizzie squeezed the squeaky toy.

Some dogs stayed put and posed for the camera.

One dog — namely, Pugsley — got up and zoomed around the room, dodging everyone who tried to catch him and nearly knocking over Katana's fancy lights.

And a few dogs lay down and went to sleep while Katana pointed her camera at them.

Lizzie laughed through it all. "This is so much fun," she told Katana. "If you ever need an assistant on your jobs, let me know."

Finally, Aunt Amanda brought in the very last dog. "This is Baxter," she said as she led an energetic brown puppy into the room. "After we take his picture, we'll try for a group shot. That should be interesting."

Lizzie had never met Baxter. He was a beautiful puppy, with a curly chestnut coat, a white chest and paws, floppy ears, and a friendly face. His shiny brown eyes peeked through a curtain of wavy hair, making him look like a funny little man with extra-bushy eyebrows. He bounded happily over to greet Lizzie, pulling Aunt Amanda along behind him. "Hello there, Baxter!" Lizzie squatted down to rub his floppy ears and kiss his sweet black nose. His soft curls reminded her of Noodle, a golden doodle puppy (half poodle, half golden retriever) her family had fostered. Lizzie had fallen hard for Noodle and he had not been easy to give up. Was Baxter part poodle, also?

"What breed are you, cutie?" Lizzie pictured the "Dog Breeds of the World" poster hanging in her room at home. Which dog looked most like Baxter?

Aunt Amanda started to say something, but Lizzie stopped her. "Wait," she said. She held up her hand. "Don't tell me. I bet I can guess."

CHAPTER TWO

"Is he a Portuguese water dog?" Lizzie asked.

Aunt Amanda burst out laughing. "Amazing! You have really studied up on your dog breeds. You're never wrong." She bent down to pet Baxter. "Yes, Baxter here is a Portie, or a PWD, as some people call them."

"I've heard of them," said Katana, "but I've never met one before."

"They're incredible dogs," said Lizzie. Now she remembered everything she had read about the breed. "Did you know they were originally bred to help Portuguese fishermen herd fish — the way a border collie herds sheep? They would swim into the ocean and chase fish right into the fishermen's nets. These dogs *love* water and they are amazing swimmers."

"Baxter is only six months old," said Aunt Amanda. "He hasn't had the chance to try swimming yet, but he does love water. According to Elaina, his owner, he's fascinated by it. He's always staring at his water dish, and patting at the water with his paw."

Gently, Lizzie took one of Baxter's white paws and spread the toes apart. "He'll be a great swimmer when he does get the chance. Look, he has webbed feet, like a duck. Labrador retrievers have that, too. It helps them swim."

"Fascinating," said Katana. "All very fascinating. But — ahem —" She checked her watch. "Maybe we should finish up?"

"Of course," said Aunt Amanda. "Come on, Baxter." She tugged on Baxter's leash, and the curly-haired puppy trotted willingly along with her over to the X on the floor. Aunt Amanda got him to sit and told him to stay — but as soon as she took two steps away, Baxter jumped up and followed her, whining softly.

Wait! Don't leave me.

Lizzie noticed the way Baxter wagged his tail: down low, with little side-to-side movements. That was not a happy tail wag. Baxter was nervous about something.

Aunt Amanda tried again, and again, and once more. But every time, Baxter jumped up before she got more than a few steps away. Aunt Amanda sighed. "This doesn't surprise me," she said. "Baxter has a little problem called separation anxiety."

"Oh, poor Baxter," said Katana. "That can be so hard. It's when dogs can't stand to be alone, right? My friend's Doberman was like that. He wanted to be with his owners, or with *somebody*, all the time."

"Exactly," said Aunt Amanda. "That's why

Elaina has been bringing Baxter here to Bowser's Backyard. Every time she tried to leave him home alone, he barked and whined and then chewed and destroyed everything in her apartment. The neighbors complained, and she knew he was miserable, so she ended up bringing him here. He's so much happier around other dogs and people."

"How do dogs *get* separation anx — whatever it is?" Lizzie asked. "And how can you fix it?"

"Anxiety. That just means nervousness, or fear," said Aunt Amanda. "Nobody really knows why dogs get it. Maybe Baxter had some kind of bad experience when he was alone one time, like a noisy thunderstorm that scared him. As for whether it can be cured, do you remember my friend Eileen, the animal behaviorist?"

Lizzie nodded. Eileen was great. She had helped a lot when the Petersons had fostered a boxer puppy named Jack, who had loved to eat anything and everything.

"Well, she has been working with Baxter and Elaina, and she thinks there's hope for him as long as he feels secure and loved," said Aunt Amanda. "She says that some dogs never get over their separation anxiety, but with care and training, many do." She bent down to pet Baxter. "Let's try one more time, pal," she said. She led the puppy over to the X and told him to sit. Then she took just a half step away. "Am I out of the picture?" she asked Katana.

"Perfect," said Katana. "Stay right there." She raised her finger and Lizzie squeaked the toy. Baxter glanced up quizzically through his furry fringe. *Snap!* "Done," said Katana. "Good boy, Baxter."

Baxter jumped up, shook himself off, and pranced happily around the room with his leash dragging behind him.

Yahoo! Yahoo! I'm a good boy!

"Do we still have time to try a group photo?" Aunt Amanda asked.

"Sure," said Katana.

Aunt Amanda and Lizzie went into the playroom to gather all the dogs. They returned with fifteen dogs who milled around, panting and prancing and all excited about whatever was going to happen next. Aunt Amanda sat herself down on the X, opened her arms wide, and started calling. "Hoss! Pugsley! Come here. You, too, Ginger. Come on, Crackers. Join us, Peanut!"

All the dogs stampeded over to Aunt Amanda. Lizzie cracked up. Dogs *loved* Aunt Amanda. Three of them tried to get into her lap at once while the rest dashed around in a crazy doggy dance. "This won't last long," Aunt Amanda shouted. She was laughing, too. "Better take the picture!"

Katana gave the signal. Lizzie waited until Baxter was cuddled right up next to Aunt Amanda, along with the other dogs. Then she gave the fire hydrant a giant squeeze. When it squeaked, every dog looked up, staring at Katana and her camera with interest. *Snap.*

"Got it," said Katana. She snapped a few more pictures before the dogs began to wander around again. Then Hoss decided that he didn't like the way Pugsley was nipping at his ankles. The big Great Dane started to bark at the little pug. Pugsley yapped back. Baxter began to bark, too, in a surprisingly deep doggy voice. Then all the other dogs started to bark — and run, and jump, and twirl around in circles.

Aunt Amanda laughed so hard that she fell over onto the floor. Immediately, four dogs began to lick her ears and nose, which only made her laugh harder. "Help!" she cried.

Lizzie squeaked the hydrant again. *Squeak! Squeak! Squeak!* The dogs stopped their crazy behavior for one second to see what was making the noise. "That's enough," Lizzie said. "Quiet down, everybody." She waded into the mass of dogs and grabbed Hoss's and Pugsley's collars.

By the time the dogs finally calmed down, their owners had begun to arrive to pick them up. Everybody was excited about Picture Day. Katana and Aunt Amanda had to explain over and over that the pictures would not be ready for a week. "Bring your check for seventy-five dollars next Wednesday," Aunt Amanda told Hoss's owner, a nice man named Gary. "I think Hoss's picture will be gorgeous."

Lizzie knew that Elaina had arrived when she saw Baxter dash across the room and practically leap into the arms of a tall brown-haired girl. He panted with delight and licked the girl's cheek. Elaina kissed the top of Baxter's head. "Hey there, fur-face," she said. But she did not smile. In fact, Lizzie saw tears spring into her eyes.

"The photo session was so much fun," said Aunt Amanda, who had not noticed how upset Elaina seemed. "You're going to love Baxter's portrait."

"I'm sure I will, but I won't be able to afford it," said Elaina. "I won't be able to afford anything. My apartment, my car, dog food . . ." She sniffed and wiped away the tears that had begun to roll down her face. "I — I lost my job today."

CHAPTER THREE

"Oh, no!" Aunt Amanda put a hand on Elaina's shoulder. "That's terrible."

Katana shook her head. "So many people are losing their jobs these days. It's awful."

"I'm not even that upset about the job part," said Elaina. "I didn't exactly love being a receptionist at an office building. But at least I was able to support myself — and Baxter. I could afford an apartment and food and vet bills — just barely, but I could. Without a job, I'll have to move, right away. If I stay in my apartment even a few more days, I'll owe a whole month's rent, and I can't afford that."

"Where will you go?" Lizzie asked.

Elaina sighed. "I'll have to stay with my

parents. They already told me I was welcome. And they still live in the big old house I grew up in, right by the beach."

"That doesn't sound *so* bad," said Aunt Amanda. "Baxter will love the ocean."

"You don't understand." Elaina burst into tears all over again. "I — I can't take Baxter with me." She sank down to sit on the floor next to her puppy. Then she gathered him into her arms and began to wail the way the Bean sometimes did when he was extra-tired or really hungry. Big, loud, gasping, runny-nosed sobs. Baxter licked her face, as if he were trying to wipe away her tears. Elaina kissed his nose. Sniffling, she said, "My parents have these two ancient Siamese cats, Mischief and Junior. They've been around forever, since I was twelve years old or something. Mom already told me there is no way she will let their lives be disrupted by having a puppy come into their home. Mom treats those cats like they were her babies." She began to wail again. Then she buried her face in Baxter's neck.

Aunt Amanda patted the top of Elaina's head. "I can understand your mom's feelings," she said. "It really wouldn't be fair to the cats. Older animals deserve quiet, happy lives."

Elaina sniffed and wiped her eyes with the back of her hand. "I know," she admitted. "But what am I going to do? I've been on the phone all afternoon, calling every friend I can think of, trying to find Baxter a home. All my friends know that Baxter is a real handful because he can't be left alone. Not ever. Not even for fifteen minutes. Nobody wants to deal with a problem dog like Baxter. And how can I take him to a shelter? He'd never get enough attention there."

Lizzie looked at the puppy in Elaina's arms. She looked at Aunt Amanda. "Maybe my family —" she began.

Aunt Amanda's eyes lit up before Lizzie could finish. "Yes! That's a great idea." Aunt Amanda turned back to Elaina. "Lizzie's family fosters puppies," she explained. "They're very experienced, and very responsible. They'll give Baxter a safe place to live until they can find him just the perfect home."

Elaina began to look more hopeful as Aunt Amanda spoke, but when she heard the last part, about finding Baxter another home, she burst into tears once more and hugged her puppy close.

Lizzie felt sorry for Elaina. She knew how awful she would feel if she ever had to give up Buddy. It was hard enough to give up each of the puppies that her family fostered, even though she knew they were going to good homes. Having to give up her own puppy was just about the worst thing she could ever imagine. Her eyes met Aunt Amanda's. "Should I go call my mom and ask?"

Aunt Amanda nodded, and Lizzie slipped away, into her aunt's office. She dialed and waited for someone to answer at home. When Mom picked up, Lizzie spilled out Baxter's story. "So? Can we foster him? Please?" Lizzie held her breath. She had been *mostly* honest about Baxter's problem with separation anxiety, but maybe she hadn't told Mom every little detail about how challenging he might be to foster.

"What about going to the Santiagos' cabin?" Mom asked.

Lizzie's stomach flipped. The cabin! How could she have forgotten? Her best friend Maria's family had a very special weekend place, a tiny cabin deep in the woods. It was a two-hour drive north, way up in the country, far away from any other houses. It was near a small lake, and there was a canoe to paddle, and a hammock to lie in, and a big porch. Maria had told Lizzie so much about the place that Lizzie almost felt as if she'd been there already. She could just picture the cozy cabin in the middle of the piney woods, smoke spiraling from its stone chimney. But she had never been there. Not yet. Maria's parents had always said the cabin was too small for company.

Recently, Maria had finally convinced her parents to let her bring a friend — Lizzie, of course — to the cabin. But when Lizzie had asked her parents if she could go, Mom had said she wasn't sure Lizzie would really enjoy being off so far in the woods, and Dad had worried about her getting homesick. Lizzie had begged and pleaded for days, but they'd just kept saying, "We'll see."

Now Mom was acting as if Lizzie *was* going to be allowed to go to the cabin. They must have decided she could go after all. "Maybe I could bring Baxter with me," she said.

"Hmmm," said Mom.

"Or if not, I can just stay home," Lizzie said quickly. "Mom, please? You have to see this puppy. He is so incredibly cute. You won't believe it. And we've never had a Portuguese water dog before. It would be a real experience."

"Well . . . ," said Mom.

"Pleeeease?" Lizzie begged. "He's really a good boy, as long as he's around people. And I can tell that he gets along great with other dogs."

"Oh, all right," said Mom. "I'm sure your dad will agree. He's on his way to Aunt Amanda's right now, to pick you up. I guess he'll be bringing you *and* Baxter home."

Lizzie let out a long breath. "Thanks, Mom. You're the best." When she hung up, Lizzie felt herself grinning. *Hooray!* A new foster puppy. And one of the cutest ones ever.

"Guess what?" Lizzie burst out as she charged back into the room to tell the great news. Then she stopped in her tracks and fell silent. Elaina still sat on the floor with Baxter snuggled up on her lap. They both looked up at Lizzie with the saddest eyes she had ever seen. Lizzie realized that she didn't have to say a thing. Elaina knew that the time had come to say good-bye to Baxter.

Elaina gave Baxter one more kiss on his head and put him down on the floor. "You be a good, good dog," she told him as she stood up. Baxter gazed at her with his head tilted, wagging his tail gently from side to side.

What's going on? Why are you so upset?

Lizzie could tell that the little pup had no idea what was about to happen. Elaina turned to Lizzie. "Take good care of my boy," she said. Then she walked quickly out of the room, without looking back.

CHAPTER FOUR

"Elaina was so upset," Lizzie told Maria the next day as they walked home from school. "I can understand why, too. I'm already totally in love with Baxter. He is the cutest puppy ever." She put her hand over her mouth and raised her eyebrows high. "Oops. Don't tell Buddy I said that."

Maria was coming over to the Petersons' to meet Baxter. Then Maria's parents were going to pick the girls up and take them grocery shopping for the trip to the cabin. It was definite: Lizzie could go. And Maria's parents had already agreed that Baxter could come, too — as long as he and Simba got along. Maria's mom was blind, and Simba, a big yellow Lab, was her guide dog. Lizzie was sure that would be no problem, since

Simba was so easygoing and Baxter was great with other dogs.

Baxter and Buddy had become friends the second they'd met. Now the two puppies met Lizzie and Maria at the door, wagging their tails so hard that their bodies wagged, too. "Oh, he's adorable!" Maria squatted down to hug Baxter. "Look at his furry face. And his coat is so silky."

Baxter wriggled happily as he kissed Maria's cheek.

I love attention. Any kind of attention!

Buddy nosed his way into Maria's lap, pushing Baxter aside.

What about me?

Maria laughed. "Of course I love you, too, Buddy." She kissed the brown puppy on his nose and petted the white heart-shaped spot on his chest. "You're the sweetest puppy ever."

"Baxter did very well while you were at school," Lizzie's mom reported. "He stuck close to me all day. I can tell that he misses Elaina, but his behavior has been perfect."

The girls took both puppies out in the fenced-in backyard to play until Maria's parents arrived. Buddy and Baxter raced around the yard, barking their heads off. First Buddy chased Baxter; then Baxter chased Buddy. Then they started to wrestle, rolling and tumbling over each other in a blur of light brown, chestnut, and white. Every so often, Baxter dashed over to the birdbath to stare at the water in it, and touch it with his paw. Then Buddy would run over to nip at him, and the wrestling would start all over again.

"It's probably great for Baxter to be distracted like this," said Lizzie. "Maybe it will help him miss Elaina a little less."

When Maria's parents arrived, Maria's mom took off Simba's harness and let the older dog join Buddy and Baxter in the backyard. The two puppies jumped at the big dog's legs, growling and chewing on his ankles. Simba stood patiently, nosing at one puppy, then the other. Finally, he wagged his tail and gave each of them a lick on the cheek.

"See? They get along great." Lizzie picked up Baxter and brought him onto the deck to meet Maria's parents.

"Hey, cutie," said Mr. Santiago. He thumped Baxter's sides. "What a good boy."

Mrs. Santiago knelt to run her hands over Baxter's coat and feel the shape of his head. "He's lovely," she said. "His fur feels like Maria's hair did when she was a baby."

"His fur *is* hair," Lizzie explained. "Portuguese water dogs need to be groomed regularly, just like poodles, because instead of having fur that sheds, they have hair that keeps growing and growing."

Maria's mom kissed Baxter on the head and turned to Lizzie. "Well, I think it would be wonderful to have this boy with us up at the cabin," she said.

"Yay!" yelled Lizzie and Maria together.

"Then it's settled," said Maria's dad. "Shall we go do our grocery shopping?"

For a second, Lizzie wished she could stay home and play with Baxter. He was such a cute, happy puppy. Also, she was a little worried that he would get that separation anxiety thing. She hated to leave him if she didn't have to.

But Mom urged her to go along on the shopping trip. "Baxter won't be alone. Dad and Charles are at a soccer game, and the Bean is at day care, but I'll be home working on an article," she said. Mom was a reporter for the local newspaper. "I'll take good care of Baxter. I promise. You need to make sure you have some of your favorite foods along when you're up at the cabin. It'll help you feel less homesick."

Lizzie started to argue that she was not going to *be* homesick, but she stopped when Mom handed her a twenty-dollar bill. Twenty whole dollars. Wow. Think what she could buy with that!

"No junk food," Mom said, as if she could read Lizzie's mind. But she must have seen Lizzie's face fall, since she added right away, "Well, maybe a little. It is a special weekend, after all."

Mom did not usually buy chips or soda or sweets. But she wasn't a total meanie about it. She did let Lizzie and her brothers eat their trick-or-treating loot after Halloween. Also, every year on their birthdays, Mom would wrap a box of sugary cereal in foil and give it to them as a special present. Charles usually ate the whole box that very day, just because he was allowed to. Lizzie liked to make it last for a couple of weeks by having one small bowl a day. The Bean ate his by the handful, spilling lots of it onto the floor for Buddy to snorf up.

So Lizzie went along with the Santiagos, and the shopping trip turned out to be fun. Simba led the way up and down the aisles at the store while Maria's parents piled a cart high with food. Maria and Lizzie each picked out their favorite chips, and Lizzie added a big container of the kind of yogurt she liked, some apples, and a bottle of cranberry juice. Then, figuring she still had some money left from her twenty dollars, she found some puppy treats for Baxter. "He's been such a good boy," she told Maria. "He deserves something special."

But when Lizzie got home, she discovered that Baxter had *not* been such a good boy while she was gone.

"Baxter's in trouble," Charles said to Lizzie as soon as she walked in the door.

Lizzie's mom did not look happy. Lizzie's dad was not happy, either.

"Naughty uppy," said the Bean, pointing at Baxter.

Baxter thumped his tail on the floor and gazed at Lizzie, nose down and eyes up.

I didn't mean to do anything wrong. I was scared to be alone, so I went looking for Elaina. Or you. Or — anybody!

"He's not really naughty," Mom said quickly. "It wasn't exactly his fault. I tiptoed out of the house for three minutes to pick up the Bean at day care. Baxter and Buddy were fast asleep when I left, so I thought they'd be fine."

Uh-oh. Lizzie looked from her mom to her dad. "What did he do?"

Dad led Lizzie to the back door.

"Oh, no," said Lizzie when she saw the giant hole in the screen door. "Don't tell me —"

Dad nodded. "He jumped right through the screen. Luckily, the gate was closed, so he couldn't get out of the backyard. But he must have been looking for one of us."

"Or for Elaina," said Lizzie. "Poor Baxter. He must have been so lonely when he woke up and nobody was here. I guess Elaina was right when she told me he couldn't be left alone for even a few minutes."

"Lizzie!" Mom glared at her. "I don't think you told us that."

Oops. "I — I meant to," said Lizzie.

Mom shook her head. Dad put a hand on Lizzie's shoulder. "You need to be totally honest with us about the dogs we're going to foster," he said, looking at her sternly. "Otherwise, how can we make sure we're taking the best care of each puppy?"

Lizzie looked down at her shoes. "I'm sorry," she said in a small voice. Then she looked up at her parents. "Can Baxter and I still go to the cabin?"

Mom and Dad exchanged glances. "You'll have to tell Maria's parents what happened," said Mom. "If it's still all right with them, you can go. This was partly my fault. It wouldn't be fair for you and Baxter to miss out on your big trip."

CHAPTER FIVE

Maria lowered her car window and sat up straighter in her seat to sniff the air that came in. "We're almost there," she said excitedly. "Smell that?"

Lizzie sniffed. The breeze coming through the window smelled fresh and clean. She nodded happily, feeling very lucky to be on her way to the cabin. Maria's parents had agreed that it was fine as long as she did not take her eyes off Baxter for even a few minutes. That was no problem. Lizzie had learned her lesson. Baxter could not be alone — ever. She sniffed again. "It smells good. What is it?"

"That's the pine forest." Maria pointed out the window as they drove by a row of tall, dark trees whose long boughs waved gracefully in the wind.

"They're hemlocks, to be exact," said Mr. Santiago from the driver's seat.

Maria's dad knew everything about nature. He had grown up in the country, and he could name every plant and bird he saw. Maria had told Lizzie that he knew all about animal tracks, too. "He can tell you where a moose slept, or how high up in a tree a porcupine has been," she'd boasted.

The car bumped along a rutted dirt road, jouncing Maria and Lizzie against each other in the backseat. They had been driving for almost two hours already, and most of it had been on what Mr. Santiago called back roads — in other words, not highways with fast-food places and rest areas every twelve miles. As a matter of fact, Lizzie could have used a rest area right around then, and the bumpy road was not helping matters. But since she was a guest and trying to be on her best behavior, she did not want to ask the questions that always seemed to annoy her own parents during car trips, the "Are we there yet? How much longer?" kind of questions.

Baxter could probably use a rest stop, too. "How are you, fur-face?" Lizzie asked the puppy, craning around her seat so she could see him. She remembered Elaina using that nickname, and she had a feeling it made Baxter feel more at home when he heard it. She stuck a finger through the grid of his crate to scratch his nose. Simba lay quietly next to Baxter in the way-back. The big yellow Lab was so well behaved that he did not need to be inside a crate. Mrs. Santiago had him clipped into a special doggy seat belt so he wouldn't go flying if Mr. Santiago had to stop short.

Baxter put his nose right up to the crate and stuck his tongue through to lick Lizzie's hand.

I'm fine as long as I'm with you!

"Where does that path go?" Lizzie asked as they drove by a wide, grassy trail that led into the woods. It looked like a great place to take a dog for a walk.

"That's an old logging road," Mr. Santiago told her. "They loop all around through these woods. This forest has been well cared for. Cutting down some trees can keep the rest of the forest healthy. That's why we have so many animals around here, like deer and coyotes and —"

"Coyotes?" Lizzie had heard coyotes howling once, when her family was on a winter vacation in Vermont. She smiled, remembering Bear, the cute husky pup they had fostered there. But in Vermont, the coyotes had been far off in the distance. She wasn't sure how she felt about them being closer. Her smile faded, and she felt a shiver of fear. "Do they — do they hurt people?"

Mr. Santiago shook his head. "No, but they might be interested in a nice plump puppy," he said with a smile. "You'd better keep that Baxter on a leash."

"I'm not letting Baxter out of my sight this whole weekend," Lizzie said. She turned to Maria. "I promised your parents, and I promised Elaina, too. She called last night to ask how Baxter was doing, and I had to tell her about the screen door. She was really upset."

"Has she found a job yet?" Maria's mom asked. She had heard the whole story about Baxter's first owner.

"To tell you the truth, I don't think she's even looking," said Lizzie. "She told me she spends a lot of time at the beach, watching dogs play. Then that makes her so sad that she goes home and lies on the couch and watches TV and eats ice cream out of the container."

"Poor kid," said Mr. Santiago. "It'll take her some time to get over having to give up that great dog." He looked at Baxter in the rearview mirror and smiled at the puppy. "Isn't that right, Baxter-boy?"

Lizzie could tell that both of Maria's parents had fallen in love with Baxter, just like she had.

"Look!" Maria grabbed Lizzie's arm and pointed out the window. "There's one of the trails to the lake."

Lizzie spotted another path winding its way into the deep, dark woods. She was beginning to realize that they were *really* in the country. She had not seen a house for at least a half hour. The road they were on was getting bumpier and the trees seemed closer on each side. When would they get to the cabin?

Then something strange happened. Maria's dad pulled the car into a little clearing and turned off the engine. "Here we are." He sighed and stretched out his arms. "That drive seems to get longer all the time. But it's worth it."

Lizzie looked around. Where was the cozy cabin

Maria had described? The only building she saw was a tumbledown shed that was hardly big enough to hold a lawn mower.

Maria must have seen Lizzie's puzzled look. "Well, we're not *exactly* there yet," she said. "But this is as far as the road goes." She hopped out of the car and went over to the shed. Lizzie followed her. When Maria opened the shed door, Lizzie saw two big red wagons inside, the kind that little kids pull around with their teddy bears tucked in. "We have to haul our stuff the rest of the way," Maria explained. "I guess I forgot to tell you that."

"I guess you did," said Lizzie. How long was this hauling part going to take? Now she *really* needed a bathroom. She heard a whimpering noise and turned to see Baxter pawing at his crate and staring at her through the car window. Oops! Poor Baxter did not like it when his person went too far away.

She went right back to the car and clipped on

Baxter's leash as she opened the crate. He wagged his tail and licked her face all over.

I was a tiny bit scared, but I knew you'd come back!

He jumped out of the car and shook himself off happily. Then he lay down and rolled around, waving all four paws in the air as he squirmed and wriggled, scratching his back on the pine needles and ferns that covered the ground.

Aaah, that feels good!

Lizzie helped load up the wagons. Then Simba led the way down a narrow, winding trail. Lizzie followed, stepping over roots and rocks and even a small muddy stream. How could Mrs. Santiago manage this path? Lizzie tried closing her eyes for a second to see how it would feel to walk the trail if she were blind. Immediately, she tripped over a rock and nearly fell. Sweet Baxter turned around as if to see if she was all right.

Are you okay? Good!

Then he charged ahead, tugging Lizzie along. "We're nearly there," said Maria.

And then they *were* there. Lizzie sighed with relief as she stepped into a wide clearing and saw the cozy little cabin, surrounded by graceful white birch trees. It was really cute, just as she'd pictured it. But right then she didn't want to linger over the view. All she wanted was a bathroom. She handed Baxter's leash to Maria and waited impatiently on the porch, shifting from foot to foot as Mr. Santiago unlocked the padlock on the cabin's front door.

When the door swung open, Lizzie peered into the dark room. Inside, it smelled exactly the way she had imagined a cabin in the forest would smell: like sun-warmed wood and like smoke from a campfire, mixed with a whiff of that sweet, delicious mustiness you get when you open your favorite old book from the library.

"Um, where's the bathroom?" she asked.

Mr. Santiago chuckled. "Well, it's not in here," he said. He stepped back onto the porch and pointed to a tiny building behind the cabin. "Didn't Maria tell you? We don't have indoor plumbing up here. That's the outhouse."

CHAPTER SIX

The outhouse wasn't so bad, really. Sure, there were a few cobwebs in the corners and the door was a little creaky, but it was clean and it didn't smell at all yucky. Golden late-afternoon sunlight streamed through a big window in the back wall, warming the tiny building.

When Lizzie got back from the outhouse, Baxter was waiting for her, straining at the leash Maria held. "He missed you," called Maria. Lizzie went right over and knelt down to give Baxter a big hug.

"Don't worry, fur-face. I won't leave you." Baxter licked her cheek and wriggled in her arms. His furry eyebrows danced happily.

I was worried there for a minute, but here you are again. Yay!

Maria led Lizzie into the cabin. Mr. and Mrs. Santiago had opened all the windows and doors, and now Lizzie could see how cute and cozy it was inside. The wooden walls made it feel like a ship's cabin, or a tree house. Mrs. Santiago unloaded a box of food, sorting things by feel and setting them on shelves or putting them into the fridge.

"I thought there was no electricity here," said Lizzie. "How can there be a refrigerator?"

"Good question! It runs on gas," explained Mr. Santiago as he set out several old-fashioned lamps, tall glass columns on brass bases. "So does the stove. But these oil lamps will be our only light tonight."

"Here's where you and I will sleep." Maria opened the door to a room in one corner of the cabin. Lizzie peeked in and saw a tiny space, nearly filled up by two quilt-covered twin beds. "There's room for Baxter, as long as he doesn't have to sleep in a crate."

"He doesn't," said Lizzie. "Elaina says he's totally house-trained and never makes a mistake. He slept on my bed last night and he was fine. Weren't you, sweetie?" Lizzie leaned down to pet Baxter, who was sticking to her like glue. He was never more than a couple of feet away from her.

"Want to go see the lake?" Maria asked after she'd dumped her duffel bag on one of the beds.

"Let's all go." Mr. Santiago grabbed a fishing rod from beside the door. "Maybe I can even catch something for dinner."

Lizzie pictured a big flopping fish staring up at her from her supper plate. *Yikes.* She'd have to be polite and eat whatever was served.

"Don't worry," Maria whispered to Lizzie. "He never catches anything. And Mom brought plenty of chili. We even have s'mores for dessert."

Lizzie followed the others down a winding trail. She tried to pay attention to the turns they took, but that was hard when Baxter kept stopping to sniff everything.

Mr. Santiago pointed out unusual mushrooms and mosses and ferns. Then he stopped suddenly and knelt down to look more closely at an animal track in the mud. "Wow! This looks like a b —"

"Like a big raccoon?" Mrs. Santiago interrupted him quickly, putting a hand on his shoulder.

Mr. Santiago looked up and grinned. "Right. Like a big raccoon," he said.

Lizzie had a feeling they were trying to hide something from her, and she could guess what it was. When she passed the track, she took a look. No raccoon had feet *that* big. That was a bear track. She felt a tingle run up her back.

"Come on!" said Maria. "We're almost there!" She hurried Lizzie along.

"Oh!" said Lizzie a few moments later. The trail

had opened into a big clearing, and there was the lake, still and peaceful, ringed by rocky shores and tall pines. "It's beautiful."

Baxter seemed to think so, too. He pulled at the leash, dragging Lizzie right down to the lake. "Careful, Baxter," said Lizzie. "Don't pull me in." But Baxter stopped short when he reached the water's edge. He patted at the surface with one paw and jumped back when the water rippled.

Yikes! I love this stuff, but I've never seen so much of it all in one place!

Then he inched forward and patted at the water again.

Cool!

Lizzie and Maria laughed as they watched Baxter. "I guess he really is a water dog," said

Lizzie. "Look at him. He can't take his eyes off it."

"Better keep *your* eyes on *him*," said Mr. Santiago. "That water's not deep, but it's definitely over that little peanut's head."

"Maybe we should teach him to swim!" said Maria. "We could lead him in deeper and show him how to do the doggy paddle."

Lizzie shook her head. "It's better not to push him," she said. "Aunt Amanda says dogs learn best when they are ready. He'll swim when he wants to swim." She didn't add what she was thinking: that the lake water looked very, very cold, and she wasn't sure she wanted to wade in.

They stayed at the lake until the sun started to go down, then hiked back to the cabin to settle in for the evening. Mr. Santiago lit the lamps while Mrs. Santiago got dinner on the table, and Lizzie did her best to be helpful without getting in the way. That wasn't easy in the tiny cabin, especially since Baxter was always at her heels.

After dinner, Lizzie and Maria made s'mores in the fireplace. The gas lamps lit the cabin with a warm yellow glow, and the fire crackled and popped. "I can see why you love this cabin," Lizzie told Maria. "It's so cozy."

Before bed, Mr. and Mrs. Santiago stayed with Baxter while Lizzie and Maria took a trip to the outhouse together, flashlights in hand. Outside, it was darker than dark. Billions of stars filled the sky, and the shadowy pines loomed high around the clearing.

Lizzie shivered. She felt very small all of a sudden, and very aware of being way out in the middle of nowhere, far away from her own familiar home and bed and the sounds of her own family settling down for the night. "You'll be homesick," she remembered her dad saying. "I'm not sure you'll like it so far off in the woods," Mom had said. Maybe they had been right after all. Maybe this hollow, lonely feeling was what people meant by "homesick."

But when Lizzie looked back toward the cabin, the cheerful yellow light spilling from its windows made it look safe and welcoming. Lizzie yawned. Suddenly, she couldn't wait to get into bed.

Inside, the cabin was warm — so warm that Maria and Lizzie opened the window in their bedroom to catch the breeze from outside. Lizzie sighed with pleasure as she snuggled down under her heavy quilt. Baxter turned in circles, then settled down with his own happy sigh on the rag rug between the two beds. Cool, fresh air drifted in through the open window, and the chirping of crickets melded with the low voices of Maria's parents from the room next door. Lizzie drifted happily off to sleep.

She was woken by a sudden sound, an eerie howl followed by wild yipping and barking. Lizzie sat straight up in bed, and in the dim starlight, she saw that Maria was sitting up, too. She felt Baxter's nose pushing at her hand, and figured that the noise had also woken him. "What *is* that?" Lizzie asked. A prickle of fear ran up her back. She knew what it was. She had heard it before. But never this close.

"Coyotes," Maria said. She yawned loudly. "Nothing to worry about. They'll stop in a minute."

She was right. Soon the howling died down and the night was quiet again, except for the sound of crickets. But Lizzie could not get back to sleep for a long time. She pulled up her quilt and lay there, worrying that she might need to go to the outhouse again before morning. What would she do? There was no way she was going outside in the dark by herself — or for that matter, even with Maria. There were coyotes out there, and maybe bears, too. There might be a huge moose or some other scary animal. She didn't even want to think about it.

Finally, Lizzie did fall asleep. When she woke up, the sun's first light shone through the window. The morning was bright and calm, and Lizzie could hardly remember why she had been scared the night before. She slipped out of bed without waking Baxter or Maria, who both snored softly. Sliding into her flip-flops, she padded to the front door. She let herself out, leaving the door a tiny bit ajar so that she wouldn't wake anyone by slamming it, and headed for the out- house.

When Lizzie got back to the cabin, the front door hung wide open. She gasped. "Oh, no!" Then she ran, her heart pounding, into the room where she'd slept.

The rag rug between the beds was empty.

Baxter was gone.

CHAPTER SEVEN

"Baxter," Lizzie whispered, trying not to wake anyone up. "Baxter, where are you?" She bent to look under her bed, and Maria's. Then she ran into the main room and glanced around wildly. But in her heart, she knew he was gone. She knew that he had woken up and seen her empty bed and run outside after her, searching for the one person who made him feel really, really safe. Lizzie dashed back to the door, hoping to see Baxter right out front, wagging his tail and happily shaking his floppy, furry ears. But the clearing around the cabin was empty and quiet.

"Oh, Baxter." Lizzie stepped inside, sat down at the table, and burst into tears. She felt terrible. The poor little puppy was probably so frightened, all by himself, far away from anything familiar.

"Lizzie?" Mrs. Santiago came up behind her and put her hands on Lizzie's shoulders. Simba stuck his nose into Lizzie's hand as if to comfort her as well. "What is it, honey?"

"Baxter's gone." Lizzie sobbed out the words. "I went outside and I didn't close the door all the way and — and —"

"John!" called Mrs. Santiago. "Maria! Wake up. We have a missing dog." She squeezed Lizzie's shoulders. "Don't worry," she said. "We'll find him. Simba will follow his trail." She bent down to undo Simba's harness. "I'll stay right here in case Baxter comes back to the cabin."

Moments later, Lizzie was outside watching Simba put his nose to the ground. He snuffled and snorted and took little running steps this way and that. He ran toward the outhouse, then wheeled around and charged down the path toward the spot where the car was parked.

Mr. Santiago ran after him. Lizzie and Maria looked at each other. "Poor Baxter," Lizzie said. She felt her heart sink. "He must have gone to check if the car was still there. He thinks we left him."

Maria grabbed Lizzie's hand. "Come on!"

Lizzie raced after Maria, but it was hard to run in her flip-flops. She kept tripping over roots and rocks. Finally, as she crossed the stream, her flip-flop came off and she stopped to pull it out of the mud. She looked at the water trickling over pebbles, and that was when it hit her. Suddenly, she knew just where Baxter had gone.

She would have bet anything that they would not find Baxter at the parking spot. Once he'd seen that the car was still there, he'd probably wandered back toward the cabin. When he'd seen the water flowing in the stream, he'd probably remembered the ripples in the lake and dashed on up the path so he could go pat his paws in the big water one more time. That puppy loved water.

Without a second thought, Lizzie put her flip-flop on and began to run back in the opposite direction. She had to find Baxter.

She was sure she knew the way to the lake: Go past the cabin. (The door still hung open, so she knew that Baxter had not come back yet.) Turn right at the big boulder by the tall pines. Follow the trail through the open area filled with ferns. Pick up the larger trail by the rocks covered in soft green moss. And then . . .

Panting, Lizzie glanced wildly from left to right. Was she supposed to take the path that led down the hill or the one that went into the tall pine forest? But wait — hadn't she already gone through a pine forest? All the trails had started to look alike, and Lizzie remembered now what

Mr. Santiago had said about how the logging roads looped around through the woods. Maybe she had started to go in circles.

Lizzie stopped for a moment and tried to think. That was what Dad always said to do when you were in trouble. "Take a few deep breaths and give yourself a chance to figure things out." She looked up at the morning sun shining over her shoulder through the trees. When she had been in the outhouse the afternoon before, the sun had come from the opposite direction. The lake was on the same side of the cabin as the outhouse. "The sun rises in the east and sets in the west," Lizzie said to herself out loud. "I haven't gone far enough to go past the lake, so that means . . . that means I need to head west to get to there. So if the sun is behind me — I have to go *that* way. Yes!" Lizzie charged down the path.

Immediately, she knew she was headed in the right direction. She thought of what her mom would say: "Lizzie, you have a good head on your shoulders — if you'll just use it!"

Soon she knew she was close to the lake — *very* close. When she sniffed, she could even smell the water. And then Lizzie went around a corner and saw something ahead: a dark, hunched shape looming large on the side of the trail.

Lizzie gasped and screeched to a halt. Her heart beat crazily. "Bear," she whispered to herself. "It's a bear. What do I do? What do I do?"

The shape didn't move. Lizzie inched forward. "*Is* it a bear?"

She took a few more quiet tiny steps. Closer, closer. Then she let out her breath in a big whoosh and shook her head. She giggled. That was no bear. That was just a big old stump.

Lizzie started to run again. The path opened into a wide clearing, just as she'd remembered, and there was the lake. The water was like a silvery mirror, reflecting the tall pines and rocks at its shores. All was calm and quiet in the still morning air.

Then she saw Baxter. The little puppy had just climbed up onto a big flat boulder that jutted out over the water. His scrabbling paws sent a few pebbles splashing into the lake. Baxter stared down at the circle of ripples that moved outward from the splash. As Lizzie watched, he took a few steps closer to the water.

"No! Baxter!" Lizzie ran as fast as she could.

But she was too late. Before she could reach him, Baxter tumbled, furry little head over furry little heels, into the lake.

CHAPTER EIGHT

"Baxter!" Lizzie kicked off her flip-flops and kept running toward the lake. Poor Baxter. Lizzie pictured the frightened little puppy struggling to keep his head above the cold, dark water. She had to save him.

"Ouchie, ouchie, ouchie," Lizzie squeaked as little pebbles bit into her feet. "Ouch!" she shouted when she stubbed her toe hard on a root. But finally, she made it to the water's edge. Panting, she hauled herself up onto the same flat rock Baxter had climbed. She looked over the edge, scared of what she might see.

But there was Baxter, swimming along happily as if he had been doing it all his life. He had a perfect doggy-paddle style. His tail stuck straight out behind him, helping to steer. He glanced up at her and shook his head. His flapping ears threw an arc of silvery, sparkling droplets into the air.

Come on in. The water's great!

"Baxter!" Lizzie could have cried with relief. Baxter didn't need saving. Baxter was fine. He really was a water dog. He didn't need swimming lessons, and he didn't need her help.

Baxter swam toward the rock where Lizzie still knelt. He looked up at her and shook his head again.

Aren't you going to join me?

"I'd love to jump in," Lizzie said to him, "but that water looks awfully cold to me."

Baxter swam away, then turned and swam once more toward the rock. He put one front paw up onto the ledge and then the other, scrabbling with his puppy claws as he tried to haul himself out. The rock was too steep. Baxter tried in another spot, and another. He scrabbled more and more frantically.

Help! How do I get out of here?

"Oh, my gosh. You can't get out, can you?" Lizzie leapt to her feet and scooted herself off the rock and into the lake. She landed with a splash and a gasp. The water was only up to her waist, but it was so cold it took her breath away. "Whoa," Lizzie yelled. "Brrr!" She reached for Baxter. "Come on, silly. Let's get out of here."

Lizzie grabbed the puppy's collar and towed him over toward the sandy beach area she had seen the day before. "See? It's easier over here," she said as she guided Baxter toward shore. The puppy's little white paws pumped away underwater until they got to a shallow spot. As soon as he could stand on the lake's bottom, Baxter stopped to shake his head again, spraying cold water all over Lizzie.

"Yikes!" Lizzie was freezing. But she couldn't help laughing. Baxter was safe and sound, and that was all that mattered.

"Lizzie!" Mr. Santiago ran up to the shore of the lake, with Maria and Simba right behind him. "Are you okay?"

"We're fine," Lizzie said. "And guess what? Baxter knows how to swim."

"That's wonderful," said Mr. Santiago. "But I think we'd better get you both dried off and warmed up before you freeze." Mr. Santiago picked up the dripping puppy and hurried Lizzie and Maria back toward the cabin. Inside, Mrs. Santiago helped Lizzie out of her wet clothes and wrapped her in a plush, warm towel while Mr. Santiago made a roaring fire. Maria dried Baxter off with another towel.

"What an adventure this little guy has had

today," said Mr. Santiago after a while. They all sat in front of the crackling fire, drinking steaming hot chicken noodle soup out of mugs. "He did go down to the parking area first — I saw his tracks. He must have peeked into the car to see if someone was in there, because there were two muddy little paw prints on the door."

"Awww." Lizzie stroked Baxter's curly coat. He had dried quickly, lying on her lap in front of the fire.

"Then, according to his tracks, he turned back and wandered toward the cabin again. But when he saw the stream the second time, something must have clicked in his head and he remembered how much he had loved playing near the water. Then he took off fast toward the lake."

"That is *exactly* what I imagined him doing," Lizzie said.

Mr. Santiago nodded, smiling. "You really know how to think like a dog," he said. "Good job.

I only wish you'd waited until someone else was there before you jumped into the lake."

"I knew it wasn't deep enough to be dangerous for me," said Lizzie. "But it was deep enough for Baxter to get into trouble. I had to save him." She hugged Baxter close and kissed his nose. "I promise never to leave you alone again," she whispered into his ear.

For the rest of that day, Lizzie did not let Baxter out of her sight for even a second. That wasn't hard to do, since he never strayed more than a few feet away from her. And when they went to sleep that night, he snuggled right up to her on the bed. Lizzie loved his cozy warmth, but as she drifted off to sleep, she worried. How would she find a forever home for a dog who could never be alone?

CHAPTER NINE

"And so, then I thought to myself, 'What would Dad say?' and I stopped and took some deep breaths and tried to think things out." Lizzie waved her fork at her father the next night at dinner. She was telling the story of Baxter's big adventure — for about the fortieth time. Every time she told it, she remembered more details. "You should have seen how fast I ran back to the lake after that."

"Right. Super-Lizzie," said Charles. "Didn't we already hear this part?" He rolled his eyes and served himself some more macaroni and cheese from the big dish in the middle of the table.

Lizzie stuck out her tongue at her brother. So what if he wasn't impressed by the way she had saved Baxter? Everybody else was. Like Elaina, for example. Lizzie had called her as soon as she'd gotten home from the cabin, to tell her the whole story. Elaina had been upset at first, but then she had laughed and cried and gasped in all the right places. "You did? Really? You jumped right into the freezing cold lake?" she'd said. "Tell me again about how Baxter swam." Lizzie could tell that it broke Elaina's heart to hear about Baxter — but at the same time, she wanted every detail.

At school the next day, everybody in class had loved the story, too. Lizzie had shared it at morning meeting. Afterward, she answered questions.

"You dove in off a big rock?" asked Daniel.

Lizzie nodded, even though it had been more of a jump than a dive.

"How far did you have to swim to get to shore?" Caroline asked.

"It wasn't that far." Lizzie shrugged. She didn't

mention that she had actually been walking, not swimming, since the lake was not deep.

"Were you scared?" asked Aaron.

Lizzie shook her head. "No way," she said. "I didn't have *time* to be scared."

At lunch, Maria was in line right behind Lizzie. As Lizzie reached for a tuna sandwich, Maria murmured into her ear, "You were *too* scared."

Lizzie stood up straighter. "Was not —" she began. Then she remembered how she'd felt when she had thought she'd seen a bear — like the breath had been knocked out of her. She sighed, and her shoulders slumped. "Okay, you're right," she said. "I was terrified. And my parents were right, too. I was homesick. But you know what? It all worked out in the end, and it was worth it to finally be at the cabin. When do I get to come again?"

After school, Lizzie was telling her mother the part about jumping into the lake all over again, when Mom interrupted. "Lizzie," she said, "sit down for a second and listen. There's something we need to discuss." She sounded serious.

"What is it?" Lizzie did not like the look on her mother's face. She pulled Baxter onto her lap and sat on the couch. She stroked the curly white hair on his chest, and Baxter licked her cheek and wagged his tail.

I missed you today, even though I wasn't all alone.

"I know how much you love Baxter," Mom began, "and how much you want to foster him and find him the perfect forever home."

Lizzie nodded. That was all true.

"But . . . ," Mom said, and Lizzie's stomach took a dive.

"But I'm not sure we'll be able to keep him much longer," Mom finished.

"What do you mean?" Lizzie squeezed Baxter,

hugging him hard to her chest until Baxter squealed. She loosened her hold.

"Do you remember that Dad is going to a fire-fighters' convention this Thursday?" Mom asked.

Lizzie nodded.

"Well, he'll be away for three days. And on Friday I've promised to be the class mother when the Bean's day care takes its field trip to Fable Farm. They're going to pick out pumpkins and feed the goats and chickens, and the Bean is really excited about it." Mom looked at Lizzie.

Lizzie got the picture. If Mom and Dad were both away from home, Baxter would be alone during the day. That couldn't happen. But there was an easy answer. "So I'll stay home from school," Lizzie said.

Mom shook her head. "Nice try," she said. "No way."

"What about Aunt Amanda?" asked Lizzie. "Can't she take Baxter?"

Mom shook her head again. "I'm afraid not. I already called her, and she says she is completely full for the next two weeks. If she takes any extra dogs, she could lose her license."

"So where will he go?" Lizzie asked.

"I also called Ms. Dobbins, and she said she can take him at Caring Paws for the day," Mom told her.

Now Lizzie shook her head. "No. That won't work for Baxter. He'll be all alone." Lizzie knew that as far as animal shelters went, Caring Paws was the best. Ms. Dobbins made sure the place was always clean and warm. The animals were well fed and got plenty of attention. But being taken out for a walk twice a day was not nearly enough for a dog like Baxter, who needed to be near people all the time.

Lizzie buried her nose in Baxter's fur and took a deep sniff, smelling his delicious puppy scent. She had never met a puppy with a softer coat.

Baxter snuffled in her ear.

I love being close to you!

Mom held up her hands. "I will try to find another parent to take my place on the field trip," she said. "But, Lizzie, even if I can, it will only put this off for a day or two. We will have to take him to Caring Paws after that. Ms. Dobbins promised me that she will take great care of him, and find him a terrific home."

"No," said Lizzie.

Mom just shook her head. "I have other obligations, too. And so does your dad. We are just too busy a family to care for a puppy who always needs to be with people."

"But, Mom . . ." Lizzie couldn't stand it. "Baxter will get stuck at the shelter forever, like Fred."

Fred was a grumpy dachshund who had a little biting problem. Ms. Dobbins had to be honest about the dogs at her shelter, and when people learned that Fred had nipped a toddler on the nose, they did not want to take him home. As cute as he was, Fred had spent more than seven weeks at Caring Paws before a nice retired man had adopted him. How long would Baxter, a puppy who couldn't be left alone, have to stay?

Lizzie begged, and Lizzie made promises, and Lizzie even cried a little. But Mom was firm. Baxter would have to go to Caring Paws. And the worst part was that Lizzie was going to have to tell Elaina.

CHAPTER TEN

It was the hardest phone call Lizzie had ever had to make. But she knew it would not be right to take Baxter to Caring Paws without telling Elaina. She wished she could put it off, but she knew it had to be done. That night, after dinner, she went to the phone and dialed.

"Hello?" Elaina answered the phone in a flat voice.

"Hi, Elaina, this is Lizzie."

"Oh, hi." Now Elaina sounded a little livelier. "How's Baxter?"

"He's fine," said Lizzie. "No new adventures. How about you? Did you find a job yet?" She knew she was stalling, but she could hardly stand to give Elaina the news that her puppy was headed for the animal shelter.

"Nope," said Elaina. She didn't sound lively anymore, and she didn't say anything else.

"Oh," said Lizzie. She had a feeling that Elaina didn't want to talk about it. "How about the beach? Have you been going down there to watch the dogs play?"

"Nope," said Elaina.

Lizzie thought about that for a second. Would she want to watch other people's dogs play if she'd had to give up Buddy? Maybe not. "Well," Lizzie said finally, because she had to say *something*, "I hate to tell you this, but my family won't be able to keep Baxter for much longer. In a few days, we'll probably have to take him to Caring Paws, the animal shelter." She waited for a second, but Elaina didn't say a word. "Ms. Dobbins is really nice," Lizzie said. "She'll take excellent care of Baxter. I promise. He'll be safe, and warm, and the kennels are clean, and —" Lizzie knew she was babbling, but she couldn't stop herself. "And she'll find him a good home, with a good family. I'm sure she will." Finally, she took a breath. "Elaina? Are you okay?"

Elaina sniffled into the phone. "I have to go," she said, and hung up.

Lizzie stared at the phone in her hand. She felt awful. She scooped Baxter into her arms and snuggled her nose into the thick fur of his neck. "Oh, Baxter," she said. "I'm so sorry."

Mom did manage to find someone else to go on the Bean's field trip, and then it was the weekend and Lizzie was home all day, so she could take care of Baxter herself. She played with him all day long and let him sleep on her bed at night. She hugged him and gave him treats. She bought him a stuffed polar bear named Snowy. She taught him how to shake hands so he could impress people who came to the shelter looking for a dog to adopt. And Charles helped her give him a bath and comb his silky fur until it shone.

Then, on Sunday night, it was time. Charles and the Bean and Dad all gave Baxter some special good-bye hugs, and then Lizzie loaded the puppy into the crate in the back of the van.

"You know I hate to do this, Lizzie," said Mom as they drove to Caring Paws. "But I'm sure Baxter will be adopted very soon. He's so cute, and so well behaved."

"As long as someone's always around," Lizzie said. "Don't forget that little part." She twisted in her seat to look at Baxter. He really was adorable. If only they could keep him a little longer, she was sure she could help him get over his separation anxiety. "I'll miss you so much, fur-face." She poked in a finger to stroke his nose.

Baxter thumped his tail and licked her fingers through the wires of the crate.

Where are we headed now? Not that it makes any difference. I have fun no matter where I go with you!

Lizzie knew that Baxter had no idea where he was headed or why. But she did. She knew that she was going to lead him into one of the dog runs at the shelter, close the door behind him, and leave him there. A lump grew in her throat, and a tear slid down her cheek. Poor Baxter. Nothing like this had ever happened before to one of the Petersons' foster puppies. Why did it have to be Baxter?

When they arrived at Caring Paws, Lizzie took Baxter out of his crate and cradled him in her arms. Ms. Dobbins met them at the front door. She had agreed to come in on a Sunday night, when it would be quieter, and she had promised to stay with Baxter until he fell asleep. When he woke in the morning, there would be people around, and lots of activity.

"Hello, Baxter." Ms. Dobbins reached out to pet Baxter's cheek. "Don't worry, sweetie. You'll be just fine here."

Baxter licked her hand, then snuggled deeper into Lizzie's arms.

I'll be just fine anywhere, as long as you're with me.

Lizzie could hardly stand it. Baxter trusted her. How could she leave him here? She hugged him closer and kissed the top of his head. One of her tears dropped onto his nose, and he licked it off.

"We'll put him in kennel number one. That's closest to the office, so people will be coming and going more often," said Ms. Dobbins as she led them into the dog room.

Lizzie and her mom had brought the red flannel sheet that Baxter had been sleeping on. When Ms. Dobbins opened the gate to kennel one, Mom went in and arranged the sheet on top of the comfy, clean dog bed that was already in there. Then she pulled Snowy the polar bear out of her bag and tucked him in. She stepped back, and Lizzie saw her give her eyes a quick wipe. Mom was crying, too.

Lizzie went into the kennel with Baxter and set him on the bed, then sat down next to him. "You're going to be fine." She stroked his ears. "Just fine."

Baxter peered through his bangs at her and licked another salty tear from her cheek.

You seem upset. I wonder why.

Lizzie laid her cheek against Baxter's. He was so sweet. How could they leave him all alone here?

Then Lizzie heard a loud pounding at the front door.

"What's *that*?" Ms. Dobbins asked.

"Open up!" somebody yelled.

Ms. Dobbins disappeared, heading for the door. And when she came back, she was not alone.

Elaina was with her. And they were both smiling.

"Baxter!" Elaina cried. She ran into the kennel and threw herself down next to Baxter. Baxter squirmed and wriggled and thumped his tail and licked every inch of Elaina's face.

You came back. I knew you would come back!

"What — what are you doing here?" Lizzie was almost afraid to ask.

"I came to get Baxter, that's what!" said Elaina. "When you told me he was going to have to come to the shelter, that did it. I got up off the couch and I went looking for a job. And I found one. I'll be waitressing at a restaurant near the beach. Not only that, one of my best friends from high school works there, too, and she's looking for a roommate — and she loves dogs."

She sat up with Baxter in her lap. "What do you think of that, fur-face?" she asked. "There will always be someone with you, since Rebecca works the early shift and I'll be working the late shift, and we'll be right by the beach, so you can play with the other dogs and practice your swimming."

Baxter sprang out of her arms and spun in circles, barking happily.

Whatever you're saying, it sounds good to me!

Lizzie wiped away some tears. She was still crying, but now she was smiling, too. She could not have thought of a better forever home for Baxter.

Puppy Tips

Can you think like a dog, the way Lizzie did when she was looking for Baxter? It's fun to put yourself inside a dog's head and imagine what he or she might be seeing, smelling, hearing, and thinking. Just for fun, try writing about an adventure, a funny moment, or just an ordinary day from your dog's point of view (or from the point of view of a made-up dog if you don't have one of your own). Learning to think like a dog will make you love dogs even more!

Dear Reader,

I loved writing this book because Lizzie got to go to Maria's family's cabin in the woods. I had so much fun imagining just what that cabin would look like (and smell like!), and I loved picturing the trails through beautiful woods to the sparkling, hidden lake. Spending time in the outdoors — every day — is very important to me. And there's no better companion than a dog for a walk in the woods, a ski on the trail, or a swim in the lake!

Yours from the Puppy Place,
Ellen Miles

P.S. To see how the Peterson's came to own their own puppy, check out BUDDY.

ABOUT THE AUTHOR

Ellen Miles likes to write about the different personalities of dogs. She is the author of more than 30 books, including the Puppy Place and Taylor-Made Tales series as well as *The Pied Piper* and other Scholastic Classics. Ellen loves to be outdoors every day, walking, biking, skiing, or swimming, depending on the season. She also loves to read, cook, explore her beautiful state, and hang out with friends and family. She lives in Vermont.

If you love animals, be sure to read all the adorable stories in the Puppy Place series!

From a magic poster—a real live pony!